DEVELOP & DESTROY: A PSYCHOLOGICAL MYSTERY THRILLER BOOK OF ERASED MEMORIES, FAMILY SECRETS, AND A CREEPY PAST MYSTERY (MISTERY, SUPENSE AND THRILLER BOOKS FOR ADULTS)

(PSYCHOLOGICAL MYSTERY BOOK 2) AN UNDEVELOPED ROLL OF FILM. A PHOTOGRAPH THAT SHOULDN'T EXIST. A PAST THEY WERE NEVER MEANT TO UNCOVER.

MARGOT SINCLAIR

CONTENTS

Epilogue	v
1. The Forgotten Film	1
2. The Cabin Connection	4
3. The Stranger in the Woods	10
4. A Sister's Search	15
5. The Missing Year	20
6. The Impossible Photograph	24
7. The Echo Facility (Utah)	28
8. The Two Astrids	33
9. The Final Tape	39
10. The Confrontation	45
11. Breaking the Cycle	48
12. The Final Image	51
Prologue: The Nature of Identity and Memory	55

EPILOGUE

The **camera felt heavy** in Ash's hands.

She turned it over, her fingers brushing against the worn leather casing. The thrift store owner had told her it was **a rare find**, an old **Canon AE-1** from the '80s.

But that wasn't what caught her attention.

It was the **film roll inside.**

A **completely undeveloped roll of Kodak film**, still wound tight inside the camera.

She stared at it, a strange unease creeping up her spine.

Because when she had held the camera for the first time, something had **flashed in her mind.**

A cabin.

A woman's voice, distorted and fading.

And the feeling that she had **been here before.**

Even though she had never stepped foot in Montana in her life.

Ash swallowed hard and shoved the camera into her bag. She would **develop the film tomorrow.**

Maybe it was nothing.

Maybe it was just **old, forgotten images**—snapshots from a stranger's life.

EPILOGUE

Or maybe—
Maybe it was something else.
Something she **wasn't supposed to find.**
And when she saw the pictures for the first time, **she would realize the truth.**
She wasn't just looking at **memories from the past.**
She was looking at **herself.**
And she had no idea **how that was possible.**

1

THE FORGOTTEN FILM

The moment **Ash Calloway** saw the photo, she forgot how to breathe.

It was impossible.

But there she was—**frozen in time, captured on film, standing in a place she had never been.**

She traced her fingers over the glossy surface of the photograph, her pulse hammering in her ears.

The negatives were old, but the images had developed **perfectly**.

At first, they seemed **ordinary—grainy landscapes, abandoned highways, dense Montana forests.**

But then—**the final three photos.**

That's when everything changed.

The first was **a cabin.**

The second was **her own face staring back at her—except the date printed along the edge read 1987.**

And the third—

The third was of a **woman standing outside the cabin, holding a cassette tape.**

Not just any woman.

Ellie Mercer.

A Face She Shouldn't Know

Ash **staggered back from the light table, knocking over a stack of undeveloped negatives.**

Her hands were **shaking.**

She **didn't know this woman.** She had never seen her in her life.

And yet—**the moment she saw the photograph, something inside her shifted.**

Like a missing piece of herself **had just clicked into place.**

A cabin. A tape.

And Ellie Mercer.

Her name sat heavy in Ash's mind, as if it had been there all along, just waiting for her to find it.

She reached for the film canister, **checking the label again.**

It had been tucked inside a **vintage Canon AE-1, a thrift store find from two days ago.** The owner barely remembered where it came from—just that it had been part of an **estate sale in Montana.**

Montana.

The same place in the photo.

Ash exhaled shakily, gripping the edge of the table to steady herself.

She had two options.

She could pretend this was **nothing**—a bizarre coincidence, a glitch in time, some trick of the camera.

Or she could **find that cabin.**

And the woman in the photograph.

The choice wasn't really a choice at all.

Because something deep in her **already knew.**

The cabin was waiting.

And so was the truth.

The First Step Into the Unknown

Ash pulled out her laptop, fingers **flying across the keyboard.**

She searched for **estate sales in Montana**, cross-referencing them with **vintage camera listings**. It took an hour, but she found it—**a small auction in a rural town, not far from the Bitterroot Mountains.**

The **address** was there.

And the **estate belonged to someone named Margaret Mercer.**

Her breath **caught.**

Mercer.

Ellie Mercer.

Her heart **thundered.**

This wasn't a coincidence.

She grabbed her bag, **stuffing the photographs and negatives inside.**

She needed to go to Montana.

She needed to find that **cabin.**

And most of all—**she needed to find Ellie Mercer.**

Because somehow, against all logic—

Ellie had been waiting for her.

2

THE CABIN CONNECTION

Ash **drove for hours.**
The sky stretched wide over **Montana's endless forests**, the road disappearing into the distance like a ribbon unraveling beneath her tires.

She had left behind **her quiet, familiar world**, trading it for something **unknown, unsettling... inevitable.**

Because this wasn't just about **a roll of film.**

It was about **something she had lost.**

Something she didn't even know she was looking for.

Until now.

The Estate Sale **Connection**

She reached **the town just after dusk**, pulling into the gravel lot behind the **Mercer Estate's auction house.**

The place was dark, the main door locked.

But a light was still on inside.

Ash knocked **once**. Then again, harder.

A **thin man in his sixties** opened the door, his eyes squinting in suspicion. **"We're closed."**

Ash lifted her camera bag. "**I'm looking for information on an old Canon AE-1 that was sold here recently.**"

The man hesitated. "**We don't do returns.**"

"**I don't want to return it**," Ash said, pulse steady. "**I just need to know where it came from.**"

The man scratched his chin. "**Estate sale. Woman named Mercer. Passed away a while back.**"

Ash's grip tightened on the bag. **Margaret Mercer.**

Ellie Mercer's mother.

She swallowed hard. "**Did you know her?**"

The man shrugged. "**Not personally. Heard she lived up near the mountains. Kept to herself.**"

Ash hesitated. "**The camera had a roll of undeveloped film inside. One of the photos was of a cabin. Do you know if the Mercers owned a place like that?**"

The man frowned, shifting on his feet. "**Cabin?**"

Something in his **expression changed.**

Not quite fear. But **unease.**

He rubbed his jaw. "**Yeah. There's a place up in the woods. Way out past the old fire road.**"

Ash's heart **pounded.**

She had expected a dead end.

Instead, she had found **a map.**

The Drive **Into the Woods**

The road up to the cabin was **barely a road at all**—just a stretch of **dirt and gravel**, winding deeper into the trees.

The higher she climbed, the thicker the **mist became**, curling through the pines like **ghosts whispering through the branches.**

Something about it felt… **familiar.**

Which made **no sense at all.**

She had **never been here before.**

Had she?

Her fingers **tightened around the steering wheel.**

The camera bag sat on the passenger seat, the photos **still tucked inside.**

She couldn't stop looking at the one of **Ellie Mercer.**

The woman in the picture stood outside the **same cabin Ash was driving toward right now.**

Holding a **cassette tape.**

Ash didn't know why, but the sight of it made her **skin crawl.**

Like the past **was bleeding through.**

Like she had been **here before.**

Even though she knew that wasn't possible.

The Cabin in the Trees

She saw it through the fog—**small, worn down, barely standing.**

The same cabin from the photograph.

Ash parked the car, stepping into the damp grass.

The woods were **silent.**

Not peaceful—just **waiting.**

She took a breath and **pushed the door open.**

The inside was exactly like the picture.

Old furniture. A broken stove. Dust layered over everything.

And in the corner—

Her **stomach twisted.**

A cassette recorder.

It was **old**, the plastic cracked, the buttons stiff with age. But it was there.

Waiting.

She stepped closer, her fingers hovering over it.

Why did it feel like she had **seen this before?**

Like she had **been here before?**

Her hand **shook** as she lifted the lid—

A **tape was inside.**

She hesitated.

Then pressed **play.**

. . .

The Voice from the Past

A burst of **static**.

Then—**a voice**.

A woman's voice.

Faint. Warped. Like time had frayed its edges.

"…**if you found this… then you already know… it's too late.**"

Ash's **blood turned to ice**.

The voice wasn't Margaret's.

It wasn't anyone she had ever heard before.

But somehow—**it sounded like it knew her.**

She yanked the tape out, her breath ragged.

What the hell was this?

How could a recording **feel like it was meant for her?**

Her hands trembled as she turned back toward the table.

And that's when she saw it.

A **photograph, half-buried in dust.**

She picked it up, her heart **slamming against her ribs.**

It was old. Faded.

But the image was clear.

Two little girls.

One of them **was her.**

The other—

Her chest **tightened.**

Because the other girl in the photo **was Ellie Mercer.**

The Message Left Behind

Ash's vision blurred.

This wasn't possible.

She had **never met Ellie Mercer.**

She didn't even **know who she was.**

But the proof was **right there in her hands.**

A photo of **her and Ellie as children.**

Taken **years before they had ever met.**

Her breath came faster, shallower.

She flipped the photo over, fingers trembling.

There was **writing on the back.**

Only a single sentence.

Scrawled in fading ink.

"**For A.C.**"

Ash's **stomach dropped.**

Those were **her initials.**

This photo had been left here for **her.**

Her pulse **pounded.**

Why?

How was she connected to **Ellie Mercer?**

How had they **been together in the past—before Ash even remembered knowing her?**

And what did it mean that someone—**maybe her mother, maybe Ellie, maybe someone else entirely**—had left this message behind?

A low wind **howled through the trees.**

Ash shoved the photograph into her bag.

Then—

A sound outside.

She turned, her body going rigid.

Footsteps.

Not distant.

Close.

Her fingers curled around the camera strap.

The wind **picked up**, rattling the trees, pushing the fog through the open door.

Ash's pulse **thundered.**

Then—

A **figure stepped into view.**

A woman.

Dirt-streaked. **Tired. Eyes dark and hollow.**

Ash's breath **caught in her throat.**

She knew that face.

The woman **staring back at her** was the same one from the photograph.

The one holding the **cassette tape.**
The one standing outside the cabin.
The one she had never met—
Until now.
Ellie Mercer.

3

THE STRANGER IN THE WOODS

*A*sh **stared** at the woman in the doorway.

For a long moment, neither of them moved.

The wind **pushed through the trees**, swirling mist around Ellie Mercer's **thin, dirt-streaked frame**.

She looked like she had been **running for days**—her clothes wrinkled, her hair tangled, her **eyes dark and hollow**.

Like someone who had been living inside a **nightmare**.

And somehow, **Ash knew her.**

Not just from the **photograph**.

Not just from the **film she had developed**.

Something deeper.

Something she **couldn't explain**.

Ellie's Warning

Ellie took **one slow step forward**, her gaze locked on Ash.

"**...You shouldn't be here.**"

Her voice was **hoarse**, like she hadn't spoken in days.

Ash's pulse pounded in her ears. "**I could say the same thing to you.**"

Ellie's **jaw clenched.** Her gaze **flicked** to the table—to the **photo in Ash's hands.**

Then, her **face changed.**

She **recognized it.**

"...**Where did you find that?**"

Ash's fingers tightened around the edge of the photo. "**Here. In this cabin.**"

Ellie let out a slow, unsteady breath. "**Then it's true.**"

Ash's throat went dry. "**What's true?**"

Ellie hesitated.

Then, in a voice **barely above a whisper—**

"**We've been here before.**"

The Proof They Can't Ignore

Ash felt **something crack inside her.**

No. That wasn't possible.

But then she **thought about the tape.**

The way the voice had sounded like it was speaking **directly to her.**

She thought about the photograph. The **two little girls—her and Ellie—standing side by side.**

And she thought about the feeling that had been creeping up her spine ever since she developed the film.

Like she was **walking in footprints that had already been made.**

She exhaled sharply, pushing back against the fear rising in her throat.

"**I don't understand,**" she said. "**How could we have been here before?**"

Ellie took another step into the cabin, her **fingers shaking as she reached into her pocket.**

She pulled out a **small, crumpled envelope.**

She **tossed it onto the table.**

Ash picked it up, her hands **cold.**

The envelope was **yellowed with age,** the edges curling. The ink was smudged, but she could still make out the letters scrawled across the front.

For A.C.

Ash's breath **hitched.**

Her **initials.**

The same message from the **photo she found in the cabin.**

Her fingers trembled as she **pulled the paper out.**

Inside was a single **handwritten note.**

The writing was **familiar.**

Almost like **her own.**

But that was **impossible.**

She swallowed hard and **read the words.**

"IF YOU FOUND THIS, **then you already know. It's happening again."**

A SHARP COLD tore through Ash's body.

She looked up at Ellie, her **chest tightening.**

"...**What does this mean?"**

Ellie stared back at her, **eyes unreadable.**

"**It means we don't remember the first time."**

THE FRACTURED PAST

Silence filled the cabin.

The storm **moved through the trees outside,** but Ash barely heard it.

Her **mind raced.**

She and Ellie had **never met before.**

But now there was **proof that they had.**

A photo. A letter. A cabin that felt like something half-remembered from a dream.

And if Ellie was telling the truth...

Then this wasn't **the first time.**
It was just the first time **they could remember.**
Ash clenched the **photo in her hands, her pulse thrumming.**
She felt like she was **standing on the edge of something massive.**
Something that could **unravel everything.**
"**I don't get it,**" she whispered. "**What's happening again?**"
Ellie exhaled shakily. "**I don't know.**"
She rubbed a **hand over her face, exhausted.**
"**...But I think we were meant to find each other.**"
Ash's **stomach twisted.**
Because somewhere, deep down—
She already knew that was true.
She just didn't know **why.**

THE STRANGER in the Woods
Before Ash could respond, the wind **shifted.**
A low **creak** came from the trees outside.
Ellie's entire **body went rigid.**
Ash saw it happen—**her shoulders tensing, her gaze snapping to the door.**
Like she was expecting something.
Or someone.
The hairs on the back of Ash's **neck stood up.**
"**What?**" she whispered. "**What is it?**"
Ellie didn't answer.
She just slowly **reached into her bag, pulling out a knife.**
Ash's **blood ran cold.**
She opened her mouth to ask **who she was expecting—**
But then, before she could say a word,
A shadow passed over the window.
Ash's breath **stopped.**
Ellie took a **slow step backward, her fingers tightening around the blade.**
Ash turned toward the door.

The air **felt wrong.**
Heavy.
Like something was **about to happen.**
And then—
A voice.
Low. Distant. **Calling from the woods.**
"Ellie..."
Ash **went still.**
Ellie's fingers dug into the handle of the knife.
The voice called again—closer this time.
"Ellie, it's you."
The world **tilted.**
The voice wasn't just calling her name.
It was **saying the exact same words from the final tape.**
The last thing Margaret Mercer had said before the static **swallowed her whole.**
Ellie's **face went pale.**
Her gaze snapped to Ash.
"We need to go. Now."

4

A SISTER'S SEARCH

The woods were **silent** as Ash and Ellie ran. Branches **snapped** underfoot, fog curling through the trees as if trying to **swallow them whole.**

Neither of them spoke.

Not about the voice in the woods.

Not about the note in the cabin.

Not about the truth unraveling around them.

They just ran.

It wasn't until they reached Ash's **car**—parked a half mile down the dirt road—that Ellie finally broke the silence.

"We can't stay here."

Ash shoved her bag into the passenger seat, trying to steady her **breathing.** "Then tell me what the hell is going on."

Ellie's hands **tightened into fists.** She hesitated—like she didn't want to say it.

But then, with **a slow exhale,** she looked Ash **dead in the eye** and said—

"You're my sister."

. . .

The Truth That Feels Like a Lie

Ash **stared.**

A laugh **almost escaped her lips**, but it died in her throat the second she saw Ellie's **face.**

She was serious.

Completely serious.

Ash shook her head. "**That's not possible.**"

Ellie's **jaw clenched.** "I thought the same thing. But it is."

She reached into her bag, pulling out a **stack of old papers and photographs.**

Ash watched as Ellie placed a **birth certificate** on the dashboard.

It was old. Worn. The paper was **yellowed at the edges.**

But Ash saw the name **clear as day.**

Astrid Calloway

Born: October 1987
Mother: Margaret Mercer
Father: Daniel Calloway

Ash felt the air **squeeze out of her lungs.**

She snatched the paper, scanning every detail, her **mind screaming against it.**

It wasn't real.

It **couldn't** be real.

Her name was Ash Calloway.

She had **never heard the name Margaret Mercer in her life.**

And yet—**the proof was right in front of her.**

Her mother.

Her birth date.

Her name.

Astrid Calloway.

Ellie's voice was **quiet** when she spoke next.

"**Mom had two daughters.**"
Ash slowly **lifted her gaze**. "**And you think I'm one of them?**"
Ellie didn't blink. "**I know you are.**"

T̲h̲e̲ T̲a̲p̲e̲ That Changes Everything

Ash's hands were **shaking** as she stared at the document in front of her.

None of this made sense.

And yet, somewhere deep in her chest—

Something **clicked.**

Like a missing piece **falling into place.**

Ellie reached into her **bag again**, pulling out **a cassette tape.**

The last one she had found.

The **one from the cabin.**

"**This was the last recording Mom made.**" Ellie's fingers hovered over the play button. "**You need to hear it.**"

Ash swallowed hard, her **throat dry.**

She didn't want to.

But she had to.

Ellie pressed **play.**

Static filled the car.

Then—**Margaret's voice.**

Soft. Cracked with age.

And afraid.

"I̲f̲ y̲o̲u̲'r̲e̲ h̲e̲a̲r̲i̲n̲g̲ t̲h̲i̲s̲... **then you already know.**"

"**I had two daughters.**"

Ash's fingers **tightened around the steering wheel.**

"**One was taken.**"

"**One was left behind.**"

The tape crackled. Margaret's voice **wavered.**

Then, in a whisper, she said—

"And one of you... doesn't belong."

The Fractured Reality

The car **fell into silence.**
Ash couldn't move. Couldn't think.
One of you doesn't belong.
Her head **was spinning.**
She had spent **her whole life alone.**
And now—**she had a sister?**
Now—**she was part of something bigger?**
Now—**her entire existence might be a lie?**
Ellie's voice **cut through the haze.**
"**Say something.**"
Ash slowly turned to her. "**What the hell does that mean?**"
Ellie looked just as **lost.** "**I don't know.**"
But Ash didn't believe her.
Because **something deep in her gut told her Ellie knew more than she was saying.**

The Decision **That Can't Be Undone**

Ash reached for the cassette tape, **rewinding it.**
She pressed **play again.**
Margaret's voice **filled the car once more.**
"**If you found this tape, then you're closer than you should be.**"
"**You need to stop.**"
"**Before they find you first.**"
The tape **cut off.**
Ellie exhaled sharply. "**That's where it ends.**"
Ash stared at the dashboard, her **mind racing.**
Who was looking for them?
Who had taken one of them?
And what did Margaret mean by **one of you doesn't belong?**

Ellie turned toward her, her voice **firm**. "**I don't know about you, but I'm not stopping.**"

Ash swallowed, the weight of the birth certificate still in her hands. **Neither was she.**

Because she needed answers.

And she wasn't leaving Montana **until she had them.**

5

THE MISSING YEAR

*A*sh sat in the passenger seat, her hands **clenched around the birth certificate** as if squeezing it tighter would make it **less real**.

The paper had **her name**—but not the one she had always known.
Not **Ash Calloway**.
Astrid Calloway.
Born **1987**.
To **Margaret Mercer and Daniel Calloway**.
The words **blurred**, like her mind was actively rejecting them.
Ellie sat behind the wheel, staring at the road ahead, the engine **idling** beneath the weight of silence.
Ash finally spoke.
"**I don't remember any of this.**"
Ellie glanced at her. "**I know.**"
"**No, you don't.**" Ash turned, her jaw tight. "**I mean I don't remember anything. Not just my mother. Not just you.**"
She exhaled slowly.
"**I don't remember anything before I was five.**"
Ellie's fingers **tightened on the steering wheel**. "**...What?**"
Ash looked back down at the document. "**I always thought it was**

normal. Some kids don't remember their early years, right? But now—"

She shook her head.

Now it **felt wrong.**

Like there was a **gap where something was supposed to be.**

Ellie's voice was quieter now. "You've never remembered anything before that?"

Ash hesitated. "**Just... flashes. Pieces. Nothing solid.**"

She rubbed her temple, trying to fight the **pressure building behind her skull.**

Her childhood had always felt like **a fog.**

Now she was beginning to wonder if someone had **made it that way.**

A Paper Trail That Doesn't Add Up

Ellie pulled the car into a **quiet parking lot** off the highway—a small diner with flickering neon lights.

She shut off the engine and turned to Ash.

"**We need to check something.**"

Ash frowned as Ellie pulled out her laptop, tapping at the keys.

She glanced up. "**You ever requested your birth records before?**"

Ash scoffed. "**No. Who does that?**"

Ellie didn't answer—she was already deep in some **online database**, scanning through county records.

Ash sighed, rubbing her face. "**Look, I already know what it'll say. I was born in—**"

She stopped.

Because Ellie had turned the screen toward her.

And Ash saw it.

Two **birth records.**

Astrid Calloway – Born 1987
Mother: **Margaret Mercer**

Father: **Daniel Calloway**
Ash Calloway – Born 1990
Mother: **Unknown**
Father: **Daniel Calloway**

Ash's pulse pounded.
Two different records.
One with her **real** name.
And one with the **name she had been given later.**
Ash **shook her head.** "This isn't possible."
Ellie's eyes were dark. "**Someone rewrote you.**"
Ash stared at her. "**…What?**"
Ellie **turned the laptop back**, scrolling through old records. "**You don't remember anything before you were five, right?**"
Ash nodded slowly.
Ellie exhaled. "**That's because someone made sure you wouldn't.**"

The Name That Keeps Appearing
Ash clenched her fists, **her breathing uneven.**
If she had been **born in 1987**, but **registered again in 1990**—
What had happened in those missing years?
And **who had done this to her?**
Ellie scrolled through another page. "**One name keeps showing up in Mom's tapes. On birth records. And in these documents.**"
She turned the laptop back toward Ash.
One name.
The same one listed under **Father** on both of her birth records.
Daniel Calloway.
Ash felt her stomach **drop.**
"**Who was he?**" she whispered.
Ellie's voice was grim. "**Mom met him at Echo Studios in Chicago. He disappeared when she did.**"
Ash's **breath caught.**

"You think he was involved?"

Ellie nodded. "I think he's the reason you don't remember."

The Lie She's Been Living

Ash leaned back in the seat, the diner's neon lights **buzzing in the background.**

Her life had always felt **a little unsteady.**

Like a house built on a foundation that wasn't **fully solid.**

Now she knew why.

Because it wasn't real.

Or at least—**not all of it.**

She **forced herself to breathe.** "If my entire childhood is a lie... then who the hell am I?"

Ellie didn't answer.

Because neither of them knew the truth.

Not yet.

But they were going to **find it.**

No matter what.

6

THE IMPOSSIBLE PHOTOGRAPH

The photograph was **never supposed to exist.**

Ash and Ellie sat in a **cheap motel room**, the walls **thin, the air heavy**, their search laid out before them—**tapes, birth records, old documents.**

But none of it compared to what Ash was holding now.

Because this photograph—**this one piece of frozen time**—broke **everything.**

Ellie had found it first, hidden **beneath a loose floorboard** in the cabin.

And the moment she handed it to Ash, her **entire reality shifted.**

She **traced her fingers over the edges of the Polaroid, her pulse hammering.**

It was old—**faded, slightly curled**—but still clear enough to **make out the faces.**

Three people.

Margaret Mercer.

Ellie Mercer.

Ash Calloway.

All standing **together.**

Smiling.

Like a **family**.
Like they had all been **in the same place, at the same time.**
But that wasn't possible.
Because the date stamped on the bottom of the photo?
1985.
Before Ellie was even born.
Before Ash—**Astrid—was even supposed to exist.**

The Reality That Shouldn't Be

Ellie ran a hand through her **messy hair, exhaling.**
"This isn't possible."
Ash swallowed hard, gripping the photo **tighter.** "I know."
She felt like she was **losing her grip on something she had never fully held.**
The **truth. Reality. Herself.**
"**Maybe it's doctored,**" Ellie said, but the uncertainty in her voice made it clear—**she didn't believe that.**
Neither did Ash.
The photograph was **too real.**
The grain of the film. The **natural shadows.** The way **Margaret was looking at them—at both of them.**
Like she had **known them.**
Like they had been **there, together.**
But the dates didn't **line up.**
Ellie was born in **1989.**
Astrid in **1987.**
And yet—**here they were.**
Captured in time.
Together.

The Hidden Note

Ellie took the photo from Ash, flipping it over.
There was **handwriting on the back.**

Ash's **stomach twisted** the second she saw it.
Because she recognized it.
It was **Margaret's handwriting.**
Scrawled in black ink, slightly smudged.
Three words.
"**Find the Institute.**"
Ellie's breath hitched. "**What does that mean?**"
Ash barely heard her.
She was **too focused on the feeling creeping up her spine.**
The name—**the Institute.**
Somewhere, deep in her mind, it **meant something.**
Even if she didn't know why.

The Address in the Darkroom

Ash pulled out the **developed film negatives** from the thrift store camera—the ones she had been too afraid to go through earlier.

She flipped through the images, each one **clicking into place** like puzzle pieces.

Until she found it.

The last photo.

It was **different than the others.**

Not a **person.**

Not the **cabin.**

But **a building.**

An old, windowless **facility—industrial, cold, almost buried in the landscape.**

And at the bottom of the photo—

A **handwritten address.**

"UTAH."

Ash's blood **ran cold.**

She held up the Polaroid and the newly developed photo **side by side.**

Margaret's note said "**Find the Institute.**"

And now—**they had found it.**

Ellie leaned in, **her eyes narrowing.** "This place... **It has to be where it happened.**"

Ash swallowed. **"Where what happened?"**

Ellie turned to her.

"Where they rewrote you."

The Questions That Won't Wait

The motel room felt **smaller.** The air **thicker.**

Ash's grip **tightened around the photo,** her mind spinning.

If this was **the place**—if this was where **Daniel Calloway had taken her, where Margaret had tried to keep them safe**—

Then maybe it had **the answers they were looking for.**

Maybe it held **the missing years.**

Maybe it could finally tell Ash who she **really was.**

Ellie grabbed her bag. **"We need to go."**

Ash's pulse **thundered.** "To Utah?"

Ellie nodded. **"If we want the truth, that's where we'll find it."**

Ash hesitated.

Every part of her was **screaming to stop.**

To turn back.

Because some things were **never meant to be remembered.**

Some things were **better left buried.**

But she had spent **her entire life** wondering why she felt like she **didn't belong in her own skin.**

And now—**Margaret's last words haunted her.**

"**One of you doesn't belong.**"

She needed to know **why.**

So she exhaled sharply, **grabbing her camera bag.**

"Let's go."

And together—**they left Montana behind.**

Headed toward the **one place that could break them open.**

The Institute.

7

THE ECHO FACILITY (UTAH)

The **Echo Institute** sat at the edge of the desert, half-buried in the dust of forgotten experiments.

Ash and Ellie stood in front of the **abandoned facility**, staring up at the rusted metal doors, the wind howling through the broken windows.

The **building was dead**, but something about it still **felt alive**.

Like it had been waiting for them.

Like it knew they were coming.

Ash's **hands trembled at her sides.**

She didn't know why, but she felt **sick**.

Like her body remembered this place—**even if her mind didn't.**

Inside the Ghost of the Past

The inside of the **Echo Facility** was worse than the outside.

Long, sterile **hallways lined with shattered glass and rotting furniture.**

Rows of **file cabinets**, their contents looted long ago.

But the worst part was the **silence.**

There were **no signs of life**—but the air **felt heavy**, like it had been filled with something before they got here.

Something that had never really left.

Ellie's **flashlight flickered as she moved deeper into the hallway.** "**This place gives me the creeps.**"

Ash didn't answer.

She was **too busy trying to breathe.**

The walls were too familiar.

The floor beneath her feet felt too steady.

Like she had **walked these halls before.**

Even though she had **never been here.**

Had she?

The Technician **Who Remembers**

Ellie stopped abruptly. "**There's someone here.**"

Ash's **stomach clenched.** "**What?**"

Ellie pointed toward a **dim light flickering at the end of the corridor.**

A door was **partially open**, shadows moving inside.

Ash and Ellie exchanged a glance.

Then, slowly, they stepped forward.

The room was **a small lab**, filled with **old computers, broken monitors, and stacks of files.**

And standing at the desk, flipping through a **yellowed document,** was **a man in his seventies.**

Thin. Wiry. Wearing **an old lab coat that should have been thrown away decades ago.**

He looked up the second they entered.

And froze.

His gaze landed on Ash first.

And **his entire body went rigid.**

"...No."

Ash's breath caught. "**What?**"

The man took a **step back, shaking his head**. "No. You're not supposed to be here."

Ellie stepped forward. "**Do you know who we are?**"

The man's eyes flickered between them. "**I know what you were supposed to be.**"

Ash felt a cold **pulse in her chest**. "What does that mean?"

The man exhaled sharply, looking like he had just seen a **ghost**.

And then he whispered—

"You're both real... but one of you isn't supposed to be."

The Experiment's Truth

The room **spun** around Ash.

She **staggered back**, gripping the edge of a rusted metal desk.

Ellie's voice was sharp. "**Explain. Now.**"

The man hesitated—**then slowly sat down**, running a shaking hand over his face.

"Margaret was part of a government study here," he said. "**Not as a scientist. As a subject.**"

Ash and Ellie **exchanged a look**.

"**She was part of it?**" Ellie asked. "**Not just protecting us from it?**"

The man nodded. "**She volunteered. But she had no idea what she was really signing up for.**"

Ash **forced herself to speak**. "What were they doing here?"

The man looked up, his **tired eyes dark**.

"They were testing the limits of memory. Of identity. Of reality itself."

Ash's **head pounded**. "How?"

"They wanted to see if they could take a person's memories... and transfer them into someone else."

The words **hung in the air like a bomb**.

Ellie's **face darkened**. "They were rewriting people."

The man swallowed. "**Yes. And one of you... was erased.**"

. . .

The Ghost of Astrid Calloway

The room **was too small.** The air **too thin.**

Ash **shook her head.** "No. That's not possible."

The man looked **directly at her.**

"Then why can't you remember your childhood?"

Ash's **chest tightened.**

Her memories **were missing.**

Had been missing for **as long as she could remember.**

Five-year-old Ash. That's where her life **started.**

But what about before?

What if she had been **someone else?**

The man kept speaking. "**Margaret was desperate to save you. But she was too late.**"

He turned toward Ellie.

"**She didn't know they had already taken her first daughter.**"

Ellie **stiffened.** "Astrid."

Ash **felt dizzy.** "Me."

The man nodded. "**You were the test subject. You were the first one they tried to rewrite.**"

Ash's **entire body went cold.**

The Fractured Identity

Ellie's voice was **unsteady.** "So what happened? If they erased Astrid... where did she go?"

The man was silent for a long time.

Then he looked **back at Ash.**

And his voice was **barely above a whisper.**

"She became you."

The words **slammed into her.**

Ash **couldn't breathe.**

"No."

She shook her head, stepping backward, but the room **was too small.**

Ellie grabbed the **nearest file, flipping through it in a panic.**

And then she saw it.
A **document labeled "Test Subject A.C. – 1987."**
Her **fingers trembled** as she turned the page.
And what she found made her **stomach drop.**
Because there were **two files.**
One for **Astrid Calloway – 1987.**
One for **Ellie Mercer – 1989.**
Two girls.
Two **versions.**
And one **shouldn't exist.**
Ellie looked at Ash, her **voice barely a breath.**
"**We weren't supposed to find each other."**
Ash's **world cracked open.**
Because the man was right.
They were **both real.**
But one of them **wasn't supposed to be.**
And now that they had found each other—
Whatever had been keeping them apart **was coming for them.**

8

THE TWO ASTRIDS

*A*sh couldn't breathe.

The **file in Ellie's hands** might as well have been a loaded gun.

Because it confirmed something she had been running from since she developed that film.

There were two of her.

Not just sisters.

Not just long-lost family.

Two versions of the same person.

And one of them **was never supposed to exist.**

A Name That Was Never Theirs

Ellie's voice was a **whisper** as she turned the pages of the file. "**They called you Subject A.C.**"

Ash swallowed hard. "**Astrid Calloway.**"

The name **felt like static in her throat.**

Not quite familiar.

Not quite foreign.

Like a song she had once known **but forgotten how to sing.**

Ellie scanned the notes, her fingers **tightening** around the paper. **"There were two experiments. Two test subjects."**

She **flipped to the next page.**

Her **face went pale.**

Ash **leaned over her shoulder,** her pulse **pounding.**

There, printed in **block letters** at the top of the document:

TEST SUBJECT ASTRID CALLOWAY – 1987
STATUS: REWRITTEN
TEST SUBJECT ELLIE MERCER – 1989
STATUS: REPLACEMENT

Ellie's hand started shaking. "Replacement?"

Ash felt **lightheaded.** She pressed her fingers against the cold metal table, trying to steady herself.

The truth was there.

Black and white.

Permanent.

Margaret had two daughters.

But one was **erased.**

And another was **created.**

And now they were **both standing in the same room.**

Memories That Don't Belong

Ash backed away from the files. **"No. This doesn't make sense."**

The old technician—the one who had given them the truth—**watched them carefully.**

"Do you remember your life before you were five?" he asked again.

Ash's **stomach twisted.** "No."

The man nodded, as if he had been expecting that answer.

"Because they didn't let you keep it."

Ash's **breath hitched.**

They.

Whoever had done this.

Whoever had decided that **her identity was something they could erase.**

And then—**the headache started.**

A sharp, ice-pick pain behind her eyes, like something was trying to **push through.**

And suddenly—**she saw something.**

Not just a memory.

Something **fragmented.**

Something **not hers.**

A woman screaming.

A dark room, filled with flickering static.

Margaret reaching for her, whispering, "I'm sorry, baby, I tried—"

Then—nothing.

Ash stumbled back, gasping.

The vision was **gone.**

But the **feeling remained.**

Something inside her was **broken.**

And it had been **broken for a long time.**

Ellie's **Missing Past**

Ellie was **still staring at the files.**

Her breathing was uneven.

Because now, **she wasn't sure who she was either.**

If Ash had been rewritten…

Then what did **replacement** mean?

She flipped through the documents, searching for an answer.

And then—**she found it.**
A single note, scribbled at the bottom of the page.
Margaret's handwriting.
"**One lost. One created. But which is which?**"
Ellie's vision **blurred.**
The truth was worse than she had feared.
Because this file didn't just say **Ash had been rewritten.**
It said **Ellie had been made.**

The Fractured Past

Ellie dropped the paper onto the desk. "**This isn't just about you.**"
Ash **looked up.**
Ellie's voice **shook.** "What if I was never supposed to exist either?"
Ash's **breath caught.**
She had been **so focused on her own missing past** that she hadn't thought about Ellie's.
Ellie had always believed she was Margaret's second daughter.
But now…
She wasn't so sure.
She flipped through **another file**, scanning the records.
And then—**she found the date.**
Ellie Mercer.
Born **1989.**
But the file said she was **registered in 1990.**
The same way **Ash had been.**
The same way a **rewrite would have been.**
Ellie **staggered back.** "Oh my god."
Ash grabbed the file, her own **breath catching.**
Two of them.
Two **versions of Astrid.**
One **taken, rewritten into Ash.**
One **created, and given a new name—Ellie.**
They weren't just sisters.

They were **copies.**
And **one of them wasn't supposed to be here.**

The Truth That Should Have Stayed Buried

The old technician sighed. "**Margaret tried to stop them. But she was too late.**"

Ellie's voice was **flat.** "Who did this to us?"

The technician hesitated. "**Calloway.**"

Ash's **stomach dropped.** "Daniel Calloway."

Ellie **shook her head.** "What did he do to us?"

The technician's expression **darkened.** "**He didn't just take your memories.**"

His voice dropped lower.

"**He split you.**"

The Forbidden Experiment

Ellie and Ash **stared.**

The technician leaned forward, voice **tight with old fear.**

"The experiment wasn't just about transferring memories."

"It was about creating duplicates. Two versions of the same person. Two realities trying to exist at the same time."

Ash **felt sick.** "So we weren't just rewritten."

The technician shook his head. "**You were meant to replace each other. But something went wrong.**"

Ellie's hands clenched into **fists.** "And now we're both here."

The technician nodded grimly.

"That's why they'll come for you."

Ash's breath **stilled.** "Who?"

The technician swallowed.

"The people who made you."

The Final Warning

Ellie grabbed Ash's wrist. "**We have to go.**"

Ash **didn't move.**

Her past wasn't real. Her identity wasn't real.

But somehow, **the danger was.**

The technician's voice **was low, final.**

"**If they know you're both alive, they'll fix it.**"

Ellie's fingers **dug into Ash's arm.** "Come on."

Ash forced herself to move.

They **rushed toward the exit**, pushing through the abandoned hallways—

But just as they reached the door—

Headlights appeared in the distance.

A black car.

Moving **fast.**

Coming **straight for them.**

Ellie's voice was sharp, panicked. "**We're out of time.**"

Ash **felt it in her bones.**

This wasn't just about their past anymore.

Their past had **just found them.**

9

THE FINAL TAPE

The **black car sped toward them**, kicking up dust from the cracked pavement.

Ash and Ellie **froze**, their breath locked in their throats.

This was it.

The moment they had **been running from** without even knowing it.

Ellie grabbed Ash's **wrist, yanking her back into the abandoned facility.**

"We have to move—now."

Ash's body reacted before her mind could catch up. **Footsteps pounded against the floor** as they sprinted down the dim hallway, past broken computers, past memories that weren't theirs.

They needed a way out.

And fast.

The Tape Hidden in Time

Ellie pulled Ash into a **side room**, slamming the door shut behind them.

The room was filled with **rusted filing cabinets, old equipment, and overturned chairs.**

Ash's **heart pounded.** "We can't just hide. They already know we're here."

Ellie scanned the room **frantically.**

Her eyes landed on a **metal lockbox, half-buried under stacks of paper.**

"There."

She lunged forward, shoving the papers aside.

The **lockbox was heavy,** the metal rusted from years of neglect.

Ash dropped to her knees, prying it open with trembling hands.

Inside—

A **cassette tape.**

Ellie **stilled.**

Ash picked it up, **reading the faded label.**

It was scrawled in **Margaret's handwriting.**

"**For both of you. When you find each other.**"

Ash's stomach **twisted.**

Ellie fumbled for the **Walkman in her bag,** her fingers shaking as she shoved the tape inside.

Play.

Static filled the silence.

Then—**their mother's voice.**

Margaret's **Last Warning**

"**...You shouldn't be here.**"

Ash's breath **hitched.**

Margaret's voice was **tired,** strained, as if she had recorded this at the very end.

"**If you're listening, then I know you found each other. That means I failed.**"

Ellie's hands **clenched into fists.**

Margaret continued, **her voice breaking.**

"You have to destroy the photographs. The film. The tapes. If they find out you know, they'll come for you."

Ellie and Ash **exchanged a look.**

It was already too late for that.

The headlights outside **glowed against the windows.**

The engine **shut off.**

Doors **slammed.**

Margaret's voice came through the static one last time.

"I tried to save you both. But I couldn't."

Then—**silence.**

The tape clicked to an end.

THE MEMORY That Shouldn't Exist

Ash's **head pounded.**

The pieces were there.

They were just **too big to fit together.**

She pressed her fingers against her **temples, squeezing her eyes shut.**

And then—**it happened.**

A **vision—clearer than any before.**

THE ECHO FACILITY, **but full of life. Scientists in white coats. The sound of tape reels turning.**

A darkened **room.**

Margaret **crying, whispering, "I love you, baby, I tried—"**

A figure stepping forward—**Daniel Calloway.**

"This one's ready for transfer."

A sharp, searing pain. **Light bending, time splitting.**

And then—

Nothing.

. . .

ASH GASPED, **snapping back into the present.**
Her chest **heaved.**
Her past **wasn't missing.**
It had been **taken.**
Rewritten.
And now, she **remembered everything.**

FOOTSTEPS in the Hall
Ellie grabbed Ash's **shoulder.** "We have to go. Right now."
Ash **nodded**, the vision still **swirling inside her mind.**
But she didn't have time to process it.
Because the **footsteps were getting closer.**
Someone was inside the building.
They **weren't alone.**
Ellie shoved the **cassette tape into her pocket**, grabbed Ash's wrist, and **bolted for the exit.**
They reached the **back of the building**, scanning for an escape route—
But the second they stepped outside—
They saw him.
Standing **between them and the road.**
A man.
Older now, but still unmistakable.
His sharp, dark eyes locked on Ash, something unreadable flickering behind them.
Daniel Calloway.
The man who had erased her.
The man who had created Ellie.
And he was **smiling.**
"Hello, Astrid."

THE PAST HAS CAUGHT UP
Ellie's grip on Ash **tightened.**

Ash's whole body **went cold.**

Because **Daniel Calloway wasn't alone.**

Two more figures stood behind him—**men in black suits, their faces unreadable.**

Like they were just waiting for the order.

To take them.

To **erase them again.**

Ash's breath was **shallow.**

Ellie **took a step forward,** her jaw tight.

"You knew we'd come here."

Daniel tilted his head slightly. "No. I knew you'd come back."

Ash **felt sick.**

Because that meant—

This had happened before.

The Moment Before the Fall

Ash and Ellie **backed away slowly.**

The desert stretched **wide and empty behind them.**

No escape.

No one to help.

Just them, the truth, and the man who had tried to erase it.

Daniel exhaled, almost like he felt **sorry for them.**

"You don't understand, do you?"****"

Ellie's voice was **sharp.** "Then explain it to us."

Daniel **shook his head.** "It's not that simple."

Ash **felt something cold settle in her bones.**

He wasn't just here to **capture them.**

He was here because something was **wrong.**

Something he needed to **fix.**

And then he said the words that made Ash's **entire world collapse.**

"One of you has to go back."

The air **vanished from her lungs.**

Daniel took a slow step forward.

"One of you doesn't belong."

Ash and Ellie **exchanged a look.**
For the first time—**they both knew what it meant.**
The experiment **was never supposed to create two of them.**
And now, the world was trying to **correct the mistake.**
Daniel **sighed.**
"**So which one of you is ready to disappear?**"

10

THE CONFRONTATION

The desert air was **still**.

Ash and Ellie **stood frozen**, the dust swirling around their feet as Daniel Calloway took another slow step forward.

He looked **older now**—his hair streaked with silver, his face lined with something deeper than age.

But his **eyes were the same.**

Cold. Calculated. **Expecting this.**

Like he had **always known they would come back.**

"**You shouldn't have come back.**"

His voice was **calm**, but there was no mistaking it—**this wasn't a warning.**

It was a **final statement.**

The Impossible Choice

Ellie was the first to move.

She **stepped in front of Ash**, placing herself between her sister and the man who had created them.

"**What do you want?**"

Daniel sighed, tilting his head. "**That's not the right question.**"

Ash clenched her fists. **"Then what is?"**
Daniel's eyes **flicked between them.** "What do you want?"
Ellie **stiffened. "Answers."**
Daniel exhaled, shaking his head. "**No. You already have those. What you really want is a way out.**"
Ash's breath caught.
Because **he was right.**
They weren't **here to understand anymore.**
They were **here to survive.**
Daniel glanced at the **tape still clutched in Ellie's pocket.** The last recording from Margaret.
"**You have two choices.**"
He held up **two fingers.**
"**Erase it all. Forget. Walk away and live the lives that were created for you.**"
He dropped one hand.
"**Or live knowing the truth—knowing you were never meant to exist together. Knowing that reality is trying to correct itself.**"
His **gaze sharpened.**
"**But understand this—one of you will disappear.**"

The Past or the Future
Ellie's **grip on the cassette tightened.**
Ash's mind was **racing.**
Erase the truth.
Or live knowing that **one of them would eventually be erased anyway.**
"**You can't erase us again,**" Ash said, her voice low.
Daniel's lips **curled slightly.** "Can't I?"
She took a step closer, **heart pounding.** "Maybe before. Not now."
Because this time, **they weren't just fragments of someone else's experiment.**
They had **found each other.**
And that changed everything.

Daniel exhaled sharply, looking almost **bored**. "**You think finding each other saved you?**"

Ellie's voice was **steady**. "**We think it broke your experiment.**"

For the first time, **Daniel hesitated**.

It was barely there—**a flicker in his expression**.

But it was enough.

Enough to tell them **they were right**.

Enough to tell them **they had a chance**.

Ellie glanced at Ash.

Ash nodded.

It was time.

11

BREAKING THE CYCLE

The choice wasn't simple.
　　But it was **clear**.
Ash and Ellie **couldn't run**.
They **couldn't erase themselves**.
The only way to break this was to **destroy what kept them tethered to the experiment**.
Destroy the **evidence**.
Destroy the **past**.
And maybe—just maybe—**they could rewrite their own future**.

THE FIRE That Ends It
　　The sun was **setting** over the desert as Ellie held up the **last photograph**.
　　A faded Polaroid of **their past selves—two little girls standing together**.
　　A life they had never known.
　　A life they were never meant to have.
　　Ash knelt by the **fire pit**, her fingers hovering over a **small metal tin**.

Inside—**the negatives.**
The tapes.
The documents.
Everything that had tied them to **Daniel Calloway's experiment.**
Ellie exhaled. "**Are we sure?**"
Ash hesitated.
Then, for the first time in a long time, she felt **certain.**
"**Yes.**"
Ellie tossed the **photo into the flames.**
The edges **curled and blackened**, the image **melting away.**
Ash dropped the **film negatives in next**, watching as they **shriveled into ash.**
Everything they had chased.
Everything they had uncovered.
Everything that had been used to define them.
Gone.

The Tape That Almost Survived

Ellie hesitated as she held the **cassette tape.**
The last recording from Margaret.
The final words of the **woman who had tried to save them.**
She looked at Ash. "**Do you want to keep it?**"
Ash's throat tightened.
Did she?
They had spent so long **trying to piece together the past.**
But maybe the past **wasn't what they needed anymore.**
Maybe it had already done its job.
Margaret had tried to **protect them.**
And now—**they were protecting themselves.**
Ash **nodded. "It has to go."**
Ellie took one last breath—**then hurled the cassette into the river.**
It **disappeared beneath the surface.**
Gone.

For good.

No More Ghosts

For the first time in **two books worth of history**, the ghosts **were gone.**

No more recordings whispering from the past.

No more photographs revealing memories that shouldn't exist.

No more old men in abandoned facilities telling them **who they were supposed to be.**

The past had **been erased.**

But this time—**they had done it themselves.**

Ellie turned to Ash.

"Now what?"

Ash glanced at the **undeveloped roll of film** still tucked in her pocket.

She didn't tell Ellie about it.

Not yet.

Instead, she looked at her sister—the person who **shouldn't exist, but did anyway.**

The person **who was proof that reality wasn't as fragile as they thought.**

Ash **smiled faintly.**

"**Now, we live."**

12

THE FINAL IMAGE

Ash knew she should have thrown the film away.
    She should have let it **sink into the river** with the tapes. Let it burn in the fire with the photographs. Let it disappear, just like **their past was supposed to.**
    But she didn't.
    Instead, the **undeveloped roll of film** sat on her nightstand for three days.
    Waiting.
    Calling to her.
    Ellie never asked about it.
    Maybe she knew Ash **needed to see it.**
    Maybe she was afraid of what was left.
    Or maybe—**she already knew the answer.**
    But Ash couldn't ignore it.
    So on the fourth day, she went to a **darkroom.**
    She slid the film into the **developer.**
    And she waited.

A Photo That Shouldn't Exist

As the image **slowly materialized**, Ash's breath **caught**.
It was a **photograph of them**.
Her and Ellie.
Standing side by side, smiling.
But something was **wrong**.
Because they were in a **place they had never been**.
And they were wearing **clothes they had never owned**.
The background was **indistinct**, blurred by motion, but the details were sharp enough to **send a chill down Ash's spine**.
The **sky behind them was wrong**.
The light was **too golden, too fractured**.
Like they were standing in a world **that didn't exist anymore**.
Like they had been **somewhere else**.
Somewhere that had been **forgotten**.
Erased.

The Full Circle

Ash's hands **shook** as she lifted the photograph.
Because she had seen something **like this before**.
A **picture that shouldn't exist**.
A moment **frozen in time that was never meant to be**.
It reminded her of **the first time she held an impossible image**.
The one from Book 1.
Back when she developed that first roll of film and saw **herself staring back at her from the 1980s**.
That had been the beginning.
And now—**this was the end**.
Except...
Was it?

The Final Realization

Ellie walked into the darkroom, her expression careful.
Ash didn't look at her.

She kept staring at the **photo**, at the proof of something **they could never explain.**

Ellie's voice was soft. **"What is it?"**

Ash opened her mouth.

Paused.

Then, finally, she whispered—

"We were there, weren't we?"

Ellie didn't answer.

Because **they both knew the truth.**

The past had been erased.

The tapes had been destroyed.

The film had been burned.

But **some things don't just disappear.**

Some things **leave a shadow.**

And some people—**some versions of people**—never really go away.

PROLOGUE: THE NATURE OF IDENTITY AND MEMORY

*A*fterword: The Nature of Identity and Memory
What makes a person who they are?

Is it their memories? Their past? The way they have been shaped by time and experience?

Or is it something deeper—something **unchangeable**, even if everything else is rewritten?

Throughout *The Cassette Letters* and *Develop & Destroy*, Ellie and Ash spent their lives **chasing the truth**—only to find that truth is not always something that can be held in your hands. It is not always written down, recorded on tapes, or frozen in photographs.

Truth can be erased.
Rewritten.
Manipulated.
And yet—**some things persist.**
Some echoes refuse to fade.

This story is about **memory, identity, and the thin, fragile line between them.** It is about the pieces of ourselves that survive, even when we have forgotten them. It is about the moments that refuse to disappear, even when every effort has been made to erase them.

Ellie and Ash should never have found each other.

They should never have existed together.
But they did.
And in doing so, they **broke the cycle.**
Maybe not entirely.
Maybe not forever.
But for the first time, **they chose their own fate.**
Maybe that's all any of us can do.
Maybe we are all **versions of ourselves**, constantly evolving, shifting, rewriting our own stories.

But somewhere, deep down, beyond the changes, beyond the forgotten moments, beyond the things we cannot prove—

We were there, weren't we?
And maybe, in the end, that's what matters most.

THANK YOU FOR READING.

If this story lingers in your mind after you've put it down, if you find yourself wondering about memory and identity, then perhaps—

It was never really gone.

www.ingramcontent.com/pod-product-compliance
Lightning Source LLC
LaVergne TN
LVHW020437080526
838202LV00055B/5231